For Ann, who makes every Christmas special ~ S S

For my pal, Mary ~ A E

LITTLE TIGER PRESS
1 The Coda Centre, 189 Munster Road,
London SW6 6AW
www.littletigerpress.com

First published in Great Britain 2012

Text copyright © Steve Smallman 2012
Illustrations copyright © Alison Edgson 2012
Steve Smallman and Alison Edgson have asserted their rights to be
identified as the author and illustrator of this work under the
Copyright, Designs and Patents Act, 1988

A CIP catalogue record for this book is
available from the British Library

Printed in China • LTP/1800/0385/0312

10 9 8 7 6 5 4 3 2 1

Puppy's First Christmas

Steve Smallman

Alison Edgson

LITTLE TIGER PRESS
London

"What's going on?" cried Puppy
as he skidded on the floor,
Tangled in the tinsel that was
wrapped around his paw.

Everything seemed different,
all sparkly, strange and new.
"I'd better find the cat!" he panted.
"She'll know what to do!"

"Wake up, Cat!" he cried. "WAKE UP!
How can you be so lazy?
This is an emergency –
THE CHILDREN HAVE GONE CRAZY!
They haven't argued once and
I've been watching them all day.
And when Mum said, 'It's time for bed,'
they shouted out 'Hooray!'"

"Something weird is happening – it started with that tree. I thought they'd brought it in so I'd have somewhere nice to pee.

"They covered it
with lights and balls
and chocolates –
what a waste!

"Then told me I was
naughty when I tried
to have a taste!"

"It happens every year," said Cat.
"It's Christmas time, you see –
A mad, enormous party
that's for all the family!

"Mum goes really bonkers doing
loads and loads of cooking.
They'll never eat it all so we can
help when they're not looking!"

"But Cat," the puppy cried,
"they've nailed their socks up
on the wall!
I really just don't understand
this Christmas thing at all!"

"Don't worry, little Pup," said Cat,
"this Christmas thing is fun.
And later, Santa Claus will come
with gifts for everyone!"

"WHO'S SANTA CLAUS?" asked Puppy.
"He's a brilliant bloke!" said Cat.
"He's jolly, plump and whiskery
and wears a furry hat.

"He'll bring us all a present
while we're fast asleep in bed!"

"Oh, Cat, let's try to stay awake
and meet him!" Puppy said.

Cat and Puppy looked up to
the stars so clear and bright,
And listened out for noises on
that crystal Christmas night –
The jingle of a harness and
the stomping of a hoof,
A muffled, jolly "Ho, ho, ho!"
from somewhere on the roof.

"Where's Santa Claus?"
yawned Puppy.
"How much longer
will he take?"

As they waited and they
waited, trying hard
to stay awake.

Cat saw Puppy's eyelids
close then heard his
gentle snores,

And just as Cat dropped off to sleep,
in came . . .

. . . SANTA CLAUS!

"Wake up, Pup, it's Christmas day!"
said Cat. "Quick, come and see!
Santa left these presents here
for all the family!"
"I've got one too!" cried Puppy.
"How brilliant is that?
Thank you, Santa Claus!"
he woofed and . . .

. . . "Happy Christmas, Cat!"